Look out, Bouncer!

Written by Richard Powell
Illustrated by Alan Snow

MALLARD
PRESS

Bouncer opened one eye, and yawned. "Good morning, Bouncer," said Bobby. It was the beginning of a very special day.

It was Bobby's birthday.

Bouncer bounded out of his basket. "Look out, Bouncer!" said Bobby. Bouncer landed with both front paws in his water bowl. Splash!
Bobby laughed, but his pajamas were very wet.

How many paws has Bouncer put in his bowl?

1 one   **2** two   **3** three   **4** four   **5** five

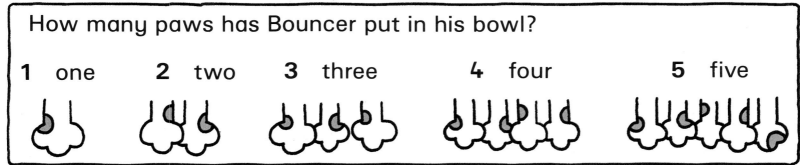

Bobby washed up. Bouncer slipped up on the soap.

Here are three pairs. How many pairs can you see in the big picture?

shoes   slippers   socks

Bobby got dressed. Bouncer helped.

What is Billy holding in his hand?

spoon

fork

knife

Bobby and Bouncer went downstairs. Bouncer went to say "Good morning" to Bobby's dad. Bobby's dad spilled his breakfast all over his clothes. Bobby's baby brother Billy laughed.

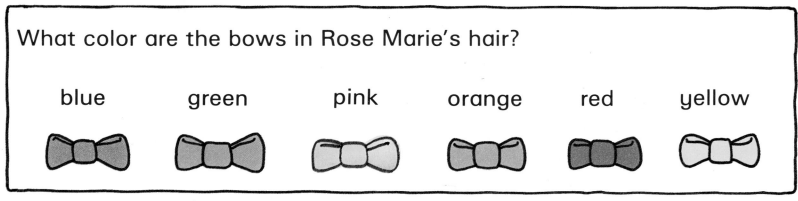

After breakfast Bobby and Bouncer went to see Rose Marie. Rose Marie was wearing her new white party dress. "It's very nice," said Bobby, and whispered to Bouncer, "Be careful, Bouncer."

Bouncer was careful, except that Rose Marie's dad was painting the wall . . .

and somehow Bouncer's leash got wrapped around the leg of the ladder which fell over . . .

and paint splashed all down the front door where paint was not supposed to be.

Bobby and Bouncer went home for lunch.

After lunch all the little boys and girls Bobby had invited to his birthday party began to arrive.

Can you see these shapes in the picture?

cube

sphere

pyramid

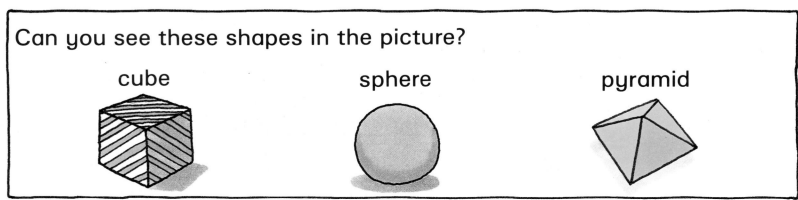

They each brought Bobby a present. Bobby loved the presents. Bouncer loved the wrapping paper.

Which ball is big? Which ball is small?

yellow ball

red ball

How many are wearing red?

They played games. Bouncer joined in playing Pin-the-Tail-on-the-Donkey.

How old is Bobby?

1 year
2 years
3 years
4 years
5 years

Everybody chased after Bouncer. Bouncer ran under the table. Everybody followed.

The tablecloth came off the table. So did the juice, the sandwiches, the hot dogs, the cake and the ice cream.

Bobby's friends said that the food was very good. So did Bouncer. Everyone got very sticky, except Rose Marie.

What is Rose Marie eating?

cup cakes

ice cream

cake

Bobby's Mom was not pleased. They all went to play ball in the yard. They lost the ball in the flowerbed.

Can you see these shaped lines in this picture?

wavy line ～～～～～   zig zag line ∧∧∧∧∧∧∧

straight line ——————   curved line ⌒

Bouncer found the ball. The children said that the flowers were very pretty.

Which fruit can you see in the picture?

apples   bananas   oranges

Bobby's friends went home, except for Rose Marie. They each took a little present with them. They said ''thank you'' to Bobby and Bouncer for a great party.

Who can you see through the windows?

"It was the funniest, best birthday party I ever had. But you are the best present I *ever* had," said Bobby to Bouncer.

What do you fill a swimming pool with?

water   mud   pebbles

Bouncer wagged his tail and rolled on to his back.
"Look out, Bouncer!" said Rose Marie.

SPLASH!